baby
loves

baby loves

by *William Lach* · *Works* of *art* by *Mary Cassatt*

THE METROPOLITAN MUSEUM OF ART
New York

ATHENEUM BOOKS FOR YOUNG READERS
New York · London · Toronto · Sydney · Singapore

baby
sits

baby
stands

baby
looks

baby
hands

baby
washes

baby
dries

baby feeds

baby
reads

baby
claps

baby
naps

baby
thinks

baby
drinks

baby
cuddles

baby
hugs

baby
kisses

baby
loves

All of the paintings, pastels, and prints reproduced in this book are by Mary Cassatt (American, 1844–1926) and are in the collections of The Metropolitan Museum of Art.

BABY SITS
In the Omnibus
Drypoint and aquatint printed in color,
14⁵/₁₆ x 10¹/₂ in., 1891
Gift of Paul J. Sachs, 1916
16.2.4

BABY STANDS
Peasant Mother and Child
Drypoint and aquatint printed in color,
11¹/₂ x 9⁷/₁₆ in., ca. 1894
H. O. Havemeyer Collection, Bequest of
Mrs. H. O. Havemeyer, 1929
29.107.97

BABY LOOKS
Mother and Child
Pastel on paper; 11¹/₂ x 19³/₄ in., ca. 1910
From the Collection of James Stillman,
Gift of Dr. Ernest G. Stillman, 1922
22.16.21

BABY HANDS
Gathering Fruit
Drypoint and aquatint printed in color,
16³/₄ x 11³/₄ in., ca. 1898
Rogers Fund, 1918
18.88.4

BABY WASHES
The Bath
Drypoint and aquatint printed in color,
11⅝ x 9¾ in., 1891
Gift of Paul J. Sachs, 1916
16.2.7

BABY DRIES
Mother and Child (Baby Getting Up from His Nap)
Oil on canvas, 36½ x 29 in., ca. 1899
George A. Hearn Fund, 1909
09.27

BABY FEEDS
Feeding the Ducks
Drypoint and aquatint printed in color,
11¹¹⁄₁₆ x 15¾ in., ca. 1894
H. O. Havemeyer Collection, Bequest of
Mrs. H. O. Havemeyer, 1929
29.107.100

BABY READS
Nurse Reading to a Little Girl
Pastel on wove paper, mounted on canvas,
23⅝ x 28¾ in., 1895
Gift of Mrs. Hope Williams Read, 1962
62.72

BABY CLAPS
The Barefoot Child
Drypoint and aquatint printed in color,
9⅝ x 12⁹⁄₁₆ in., ca. 1898
H. O. Havemeyer Collection, Bequest of
Mrs. H. O. Havemeyer, 1929
29.107.98

BABY NAPS
Mother and Child
Pastel on wove paper, mounted on canvas,
26⅝ x 22½ in., 1914
H. O. Havemeyer Collection, Bequest of
Mrs. H. O. Havemeyer, 1929
29.100.50

BABY THINKS
Young Mother Sewing
Oil on canvas, 36⅜ x 29 in., ca. 1900
H. O. Havemeyer Collection, Bequest of
Mrs. H. O. Havemeyer, 1929
29.100.48

BABY DRINKS
Mother Feeding Child
Pastel on wove paper, mounted on canvas,
25½ x 32 in., 1898
From the Collection of James Stillman,
Gift of Dr. Ernest G. Stillman, 1922
22.16.22

BABY CUDDLES
Nurse and Child
Pastel on wove paper (originally blue),
mounted on canvas, 31½ x 26¼ in., 1897
Gift of Mrs. Ralph J. Hines, 1960
60.181

BABY HUGS
Maternal Caress
Drypoint and aquatint printed in color,
14⅜ x 10⁹⁄₁₆ in., 1891
Gift of Paul J. Sachs, 1916
16.2.5

BABY KISSES
Mother's Kiss
Drypoint and aquatint printed in color,
13⅝ x 8¹⁵⁄₁₆ in., ca. 1891
Gift of Paul J. Sachs, 1916
16.2.10

BABY LOVES
Mother and Child with a Rose Scarf
Oil on canvas, 46 x 35½ in., ca. 1908
Bequest of Miss Adelaide Milton de Groot
(1876-1967), 1967
67.187.122

COVER AND ENDPAPER DESIGN: From a detail of a wild-aster textile
Possibly Associated Artists (American, New York, 1883-1900)
Discharge-printed cotton denim with silk embroidery
THE METROPOLITAN MUSEUM OF ART
Gift of Robert L. Isaacson, in memory of Gustava Harris Nathan, 1989   1989.65

Published by The Metropolitan Museum of Art and Atheneum Books for Young Readers

Atheneum Books for Young Readers
An imprint of Simon & Schuster Children's Publishing Division
1230 Avenue of the Americas, New York, New York   10020

Visit the Museum's Web site: www.metmuseum.org
Visit Simon & Schuster's Web site: www.SimonSaysKids.com

First Edition
Printed in Hong Kong
11 10 09 08 07 06 05 04 03 02   5 4 3 2 1

Produced by the Department of Special Publications, The Metropolitan Museum of Art:
Robie Rogge, Publishing Manager; William Lach, Project Editor; Anna Raff, Designer; Elizabeth Stoneman,
Production Manager.
All photography by The Metropolitan Museum of Art Photograph Studio.

Library of Congress Cataloging-in-Publication Data

Lach, William, 1968–
    Baby loves / by William Lach ; works of art by Mary Cassatt.
        p. cm.
    Summary: Presents a simple rhyme about a baby's activities, such as drinking, napping,
and hugging, accompanied by paintings, prints, and pastels by American Impressionist Mary Cassatt.
Includes facts about the artwork.
    ISBN 1-58839-052-7 (MMA) – ISBN 0-689-85340-8 (Atheneum)
        [1. Babies–Fiction. 2. Stories in rhyme.] I. Cassatt, Mary, 1844–1926, ill. II. Title.

PZ8.3.L113 Bab 2002
[E]–dc21   2002019034